## Welcome to ALADDIN QUIX!

If you are looking for fast, fun-to-read stories with colorful characters, lots of kid-friendly humor, easy-to-follow action, entertaining story lines, and lively illustrations, then **ALADDIN QUIX** is for you!

But wait, there's more!

If you're also looking for stories with tables of contents; word lists; about-the-book questions; 64, 80, or 96 pages; short chapters; short paragraphs; and large fonts, then **ALADDIN QUIX** is *definitely* for you!

**ALADDIN QUIX:** The next step between ready to reads and longer, more challenging chapter books, for readers five to eight years old.

# Rockin' Rockets

**Read more ALADDIN QUIX books!**

By Stephanie Calmenson

*Our Principal Is a Frog!*
*Our Principal Is a Wolf!*
*Our Principal's in His Underwear!*
*Our Principal Breaks a Spell!*

The Adventures of Allie and Amy
By Stephanie Calmenson and Joanna Cole

Book 1: *The Best Friend Plan*

# The Adventures of
# ALLIE and AMY

## Rockin' Rockets

By Stephanie Calmenson and Joanna Cole
Illustrated by James Burks

## ALADDIN QUIX

New York  London  Toronto  Sydney  New Delhi

ALADDIN QUIX
Simon & Schuster Children's Publishing Division
1230 Avenue of the Americas, New York, New York 10020
First Aladdin QUIX hardcover edition May 2020
Text copyright © 1997 by Joanna Cole and Stephanie Calmenson
Illustrations copyright © 2020 by James Burks
The text of this book was originally published
in slightly different form as *Rockin' Reptiles* (1997).
Also available in an Aladdin QUIX paperback edition.
All rights reserved, including the right of reproduction in whole or in part in any form.
ALADDIN and the related marks and colophon
are trademarks of Simon & Schuster, Inc.
For information about special discounts for bulk purchases, please contact
Simon & Schuster Special Sales at 1-866-506-1949 or business@simonandschuster.com.
The Simon & Schuster Speakers Bureau can bring authors to your live event. For more
information or to book an event contact the Simon & Schuster Speakers Bureau
at 1-866-248-3049 or visit our website at www.simonspeakers.com.
Designed by Heather Palisi
The illustrations for this book were rendered digitally.
The text of this book was set in Archer Medium.
Manufactured in the United States of America 0420 LAK
2 4 6 8 10 9 7 5 3 1
Library of Congress Control Number 2019954204
ISBN 978-1-5344-5254-1 (hc)
ISBN 978-1-5344-5253-4 (pbk)
ISBN 978-1-5344-5255-8 (eBook)

To Nate and Sloane Langer

# Cast of Characters

**Allie Anderson:** Amy Cooper's best friend

**Amy Cooper:** Allie Anderson's best friend

**Gracie Barnes:** Bouncy, bubbly, riddle-telling friend of Allie and Amy

**Marvin Lopez:** A boy who's sometimes fun and sometimes annoying

**Madame Lulu:** Fortune-teller who is really Mrs. Suzie Tompkins, a neighbor in Allie's building

# Contents

# 1

## *Ring! Ring!*

***Ring! Ring!*** Early one morning the telephone rang at **Allie's** house. Allie's father answered it.

"It's for you, Allie!" he called. "It's **Amy**."

**"I knew that!"** said Allie.

She jumped out of bed and ran for the phone.

Allie Anderson and Amy Cooper were best friends. They lived in apartment buildings next door to each other. When they were not together, they were talking on the phone.

"Quick. Look out your window," said Amy. "There's a moving van."

"I wonder who's moving in," said Allie.

"We're about to find out," said Amy as the movers opened the

back of the van. The first thing

that came out was a bed. On the

headboard, in great big letters, it said GRACIE. Next the movers set a bookcase on the sidewalk. It said GRACIE too. It was followed by a bulletin board that said GRACIE in six colors across the top.

"I wonder what our new neighbor's name is," said Allie.

"**HA, HA!** Very funny!" said Amy. "Hurry up and get ready. I'll meet you downstairs."

As Allie threw on her clothes, her head was swimming with questions. *I wonder if **Gracie** is nice. I wonder if Gracie likes jumping rope and eating pineapple pizza.*

As she gobbled down her breakfast, Allie thought, *I wonder if Gracie likes the Rockin' Rockets band.*

Allie raced for the elevator. She lived on the sixth floor of her building.

When she got in, she pressed the button for the first floor. The numbers lit up. *Six, five, four, three, two, one.*

Amy lived on the sixth floor of *her* building. At the very same time as Allie, she pressed the button for the first floor. *Six, five, four, three, two, one.*

Allie and Amy burst out of their buildings just as a car pulled up to the curb. Inside was a girl in a T-shirt with big letters across the front. The letters spelled out "GRACIE." The girl opened the car door and jumped out.

"Hi. I'm Gracie," she said.

"Oh, really?" said Allie, trying not to laugh.

"Be nice," Amy whispered to Allie. She turned to Gracie and said, "Hi. I'm Amy, and this is Allie. **Welcome to Spring Street!**"

# 2

## Sold Out!

The movers took a **trampoline** out of the van. "Ooh, that looks like fun," said Allie.

"Want to try it?" asked Gracie.

"Sure," Allie said, kicking off her shoes.

She stepped onto the trampoline. *Boing, boing, boing!* She went
up and down and up and down.

**"My turn!"** said Amy.

*Boing, boing, boing!*

It was Gracie's turn next.

**Boing, boing, boing!**

While she was bouncing, Gracie called out a riddle. "What season is it when you're on a trampoline?"

Without waiting for an answer, she called, **"Springtime!"** Gracie loved to bounce, and she loved to tell riddles.

"Sorry to break up the fun," called Gracie's mother, "but we need to go in and unpack."

"Maybe we can meet up later," Gracie called, running inside.

"Gracie sure is fun," said Amy.

"She sure is bouncy," said Allie.

The girls started walking down the block to the corner store.

**"Look at that!"** said Amy. She pointed to a big sign posted on a tree. It said:

ROCKIN' ROCKETS
CONCERT
PEABODY PALACE
FRIDAY, 8 P.M.

"**Wow!** Our favorite group," cried Allie. "Maybe we can go to the concert."

They started to sing the Rockin' Rockets hit song "Party Tonight."

*"Get ready for fun.*
*Get your hair just right.*
*Get ready to get happy.*
*There's a party tonight!*
*Yeah, we'll party tonight!"*

Allie and Amy knew all the words and were dancing along

when a motorcycle *vroomed* up.
The rider, who had pink and blue
spiky hair, walked up to the tree
and slapped a sticker over the
Rockin' Rockets concert sign.
The sticker said:

# SOLD OUT

Allie and Amy stopped singing
and stared at the sign.

"**WHAT?!** Does that mean
we won't get to go?" said Amy.

"There must be a way to get

just *two* tickets," said Allie.

They wanted to ask the motorcycle rider, but with another loud *vroom*, she was gone.

**Whoosh!**

A skateboard whizzed by.

**Whoosh!**

It whizzed back in the other direction.

It was a boy named **Marvin**. Allie and Amy sometimes had fun with him. Other times, they found him super annoying.

"Wow, the tickets are all sold

out," said Marvin. "I'm glad I already got mine."

"**Wait a minute!** *You* have tickets to the Rockin' Rockets concert?" asked Allie.

"I sure do," said Marvin. "Don't you?"

"Not yet," said Amy.

"You mean not *ever*," said Marvin. He started singing to the tune of "Party Tonight":

*"Boo-hoo, boo-hoo!*
*No Rockets for you."*

★ 16 ★

"Mr. Marvin Q. Smarty-Pants, you are being very **obnoxious**, and we do not associate with obnoxious creatures, do we, Amy?" said Allie.

"No, we do not," Amy answered. The girls put their noses in the air and stomped home. Marvin passed them on his skateboard several times, humming every Rockin' Rockets tune he knew.

"I can't believe Marvin has a ticket and we don't," said Allie when they reached their buildings.

"Me neither. **It's not fair!**" said Amy.

"See you later, alligator," sighed Allie.

"In a while, crocodile," sighed Amy.

They went into their buildings humming another Rockin' Rockets song. It was called "I Got the Boo-Hoo Blues."

# 3

## Movie Stars

***Ring! Ring!*** Two days later the phone rang at Allie's house.

**"I'll get it!"** Allie called to her mother. "Maybe it's Amy. Maybe she got tickets."

Allie answered the phone like a

radio **announcer**. "Rockin' Rockets **headquarters**!"

"May I please speak to Allie?" said a voice.

**Oops!** It wasn't Amy's voice.

"Who is this?" asked Allie.

"It's Gracie, your new neighbor," said the voice. "Do you want to come over? I just got a jewelry-making set. We could make necklaces and bracelets."

"I love making jewelry. Can Amy come too?" asked Allie.

"I only have enough beads

for two of us," said Gracie.

"Then I'm not sure . . . ," said Allie. She was trying to decide if she should go without Amy.

"We'll have fun," said Gracie. "I have all kinds of beads. Round ones, square ones. Red ones, purple ones—"

**"Purple's my favorite!"** said Allie.

"The purple beads have silver sparkles," said Gracie.

**"I'm on my way!"** said Allie.

She zipped out the door and up one flight. Gracie lived in the apartment right above Allie's.

"I've got everything ready," said Gracie, bouncing off to her room. The jewelry-making set was spread out on a table.

"Want to hear a necklace riddle?" asked Gracie. Without waiting for an answer, she said, "What did one necklace say to the other?"

"I don't know. What?" asked Allie.

"It said, 'Do you want to hang around together?'" said Gracie.

Allie laughed and started stringing purple beads with silver sparkles. Gracie's necklace was red and blue.

When they had finished, they each made a matching bracelet, then posed in front of the mirror.

"Who are those **glamorous** girls?" asked Gracie.

"Are they movie stars?" asked Allie. **"No, wait! They're us!"**

They wore their jewelry while they had a snack. "Guess what?" said Gracie. "I'm going with my mom to the Rockin' Rockets concert on Friday."

"Wow, you are so lucky!" said Allie.

"Aren't you going too?" asked
Gracie.

"I want to, but the concert's
sold out," said Allie.

"My mom might have an extra
ticket," said Gracie. "If she does,
I'll ask if you can come."

**"I'd love that!"** said Allie. She was so excited that she started bouncing up and down— just like Gracie.

When they'd finished their snack, Allie thanked Gracie and bounced all the way home with Rockin' Rockets tunes swirling in her head.

# 4

## Yum!

***Ring! Ring!*** Late that afternoon, the phone rang at Amy's house.

"I'll get it," said Amy, thinking it was Allie. But it wasn't. It was Gracie.

"Do you want to come over and bake cookies?" asked Gracie.

"That sounds like fun," said Amy. "Can Allie come too?"

"I'm only allowed to invite one guest for baking," said Gracie. "Do you like oatmeal chocolate chip cookies?"

"Ooh, I love them," said Amy. **"I'll be right over!"**

Gracie and Amy mixed up a bowl of cookie dough. Then they took turns spooning the dough onto a cookie sheet.

When the girls were ready to bake, Gracie's mother came into the kitchen to help them with the oven.

"This batter looks perfect," she said.

"Here's a perfect baking joke," said Gracie. "Why did the cookie

go to the doctor?" Without waiting for an answer, she said, **"Because it felt crummy!"**

"You're funny," said Amy, giggling.

When the cookies were ready, they each ate two. They helped clean up, then went to Gracie's room to listen to music.

Gracie turned on her favorite station, and the very first song was Rockin' Rockets' "Party Tonight."

Amy felt blue hearing it. "I

wish I could go to their concert on Friday," she said.

"My mom and I are going," said Gracie. "Do you want to come with us?"

The minute Gracie had asked the question, she knew it was a mistake. She thought her mom *might* have one extra ticket, but she had already asked Allie.

Before Gracie could take it back, Amy cried out, **"I'd love to go!"**

"Um, well, I can't disturb my mom now because she's busy, but I'll ask her later," said Gracie. She hoped her mom had an extra ticket and could somehow get another.

"Thanks!" said Amy. "I've got to get home for dinner. But let me know as soon as you find out."

"Sure. Take cookies for dessert," said Gracie. She went to the kitchen and put a few into a bag.

Amy was walking out of the building munching on a cookie when she saw Allie coming in.

**"Allie!"** said Amy, jumping back.

**"Amy!"** said Allie, stepping forward. She noticed Amy's cookie.

"Yum. That looks homemade," Allie said. "Where's it from?"

"I made cookies with Gracie," said Amy. Amy noticed Allie's jewelry. "Where'd you get the necklace and bracelet?" she asked.

"I made them with Gracie," said Allie.

Suddenly they both got very quiet.

*Making jewelry is really fun,* thought Amy. *I wonder why I wasn't invited.*

At the same time, Allie was wondering why she hadn't been invited to make cookies.

They each wondered if Gracie was trying to be best friends with the other.

Heading home, they tried to push down their worried feelings. After all, they had been best friends forever. Nothing could come between them. . . . Could it?

# 5

## First Fight

The next morning Allie and Amy met outside and went to the park. Allie tied her jump rope to a fence and turned it while Amy jumped, and together they **chanted**:

*"We're shakin' up the town,*
*jumpin' on the street.*
*Left foot. Right foot.*
*Now both feet!"*

While Amy was jumping, Gracie came by.

"I'll turn the other end," she said, untying the rope from the fence.

As soon as the girls saw Gracie, their friendship worries came back.

But their excitement took over,

remembering Gracie's invitation to the concert. Without thinking, they blurted out at the same time, "Does your mother have an extra ticket for me?"

Allie and Amy looked at each other in **amazement**.

"She invited you?" said Allie.

"She invited you?" said Amy.

Then they looked at Gracie, who'd started bouncing up and down.

"I—I can explain everything," she said.

**"You asked me to the concert!"** said Allie, stamping her foot.

"You asked me to the concert," said Amy, with her hand on her hip.

"Okay, okay. So I made a teeny tiny mistake," said Gracie. "I was having such a good time with each of you that I wanted both of you to come."

"How could we both go when you might have only one ticket?" said Allie, getting madder by the minute.

"I forgot about that when I asked," said Gracie. "Then I figured my mother could get a second ticket."

"So, does she have two extra

tickets for us?" asked Amy in an **exasperated** voice.

"She has one extra but can't get another one. I'm sorry," said Gracie.

"Now what?" said Allie. "Which one of us gets to go?"

Gracie looked at Allie, then at Amy, then back to Allie. Her feet were bouncing up and down. Her head was bouncing left and right.

"**I can't decide!** I like you both. You have to decide," said

Gracie, flapping her arms.

Allie turned to Amy and said, "I bet Gracie asked me first, so I should go."

"Even if she asked you first, it wouldn't mean she likes you better," said Amy.

"Maybe so," said Allie, starting to feel mad at Amy. "But as the saying goes, 'First to know is the one to go.'"

"I never heard that before," said Amy.

"Me neither," said Gracie.

"That's because I just made it up," said Allie.

**"Then it doesn't count!"** said Amy.

*Whoosh!* Marvin whizzed by. He noticed the looks on the girls' faces, then turned around and whizzed back.

"What's going on?" he asked.

"We're talking about tickets for the concert," said Amy.

"It is business that does not **concern** you," said Allie.

"Give it up," said Marvin. "The

tickets are sold out. **Gone! History!**"

"Um, not exactly," said Gracie. "I have an extra one."

"Just one extra ticket?" said

Marvin. "Who's going to get it?"

**"It's going to be me!"**

said Allie, looking right at Amy.

**"It's going to be me!"**

said Amy, looking right back.

"Wait!" said Gracie, bouncing faster than ever. "Don't have a fight! Not because of me."

"Don't worry," Marvin said to Gracie. "They're best friends. Together-forever friends. They never fight."

But when Marvin turned back to Allie and Amy, the girls were **glaring** at each other, and their cheeks had turned bright pink.

"Uh-oh. I take it back," said Marvin. **"Their first-ever**

fight has begun!"

"I'll go see if I can get one more ticket," said Gracie, running off.

"I want to hear Rockin' Rockets so badly," said Amy.

"Maybe you just want to be with Gracie," said Allie.

"What about you?" said Amy. "You made fancy jewelry with her. Now you're trying to go to the concert with her. Why don't you just be best friends with her?"

"Look who's talking. If I'm not mistaken, you're the one who made cookies with Gracie," said Allie. "I bet you'll eat your cookies at the concert together."

"I bet you'll wear your jewelry at the concert together," said Amy.

**"I bet I'm not talking to you anymore!"** said Allie.

**"I bet I'm not talking to you, either!"** said Amy.

The girls turned their backs, put their noses in the air, and stomped off in opposite directions.

# 6

## Madame Lulu

Allie's head was swimming with questions as she left the park.

Did Amy want to be best friends with Gracie? Would she go to the concert and leave Allie behind?

Would Allie have to sit home alone for the rest of her life?

Allie walked around the block to cool off, then headed toward Madame Lulu's Fortune-Telling Parlor. If anyone had the answers to Allie's questions, it was **Madame Lulu**.

When Allie got there, she stopped short. The fortune-telling **parlor** was pink and yellow outside, but it was dark and spooky inside. Even though she knew that Madame Lulu was really her nice neighbor Mrs. Tompkins, Allie was still scared to go in all by herself. She and Amy always walked in together.

Suddenly she heard Madame Lulu's husky voice calling out to her, **"Greetings! Come right in, fortune seeker!"**

*Clink! Clink!* Allie could hear the *clink* of Madame Lulu's bracelets as she waved Allie inside. Madame Lulu always wore about twenty bracelets on each arm. They clinked together whenever she moved.

Allie pushed her way through the beaded curtain. When Allie's eyes got used to the dark, she noticed that someone was standing next to her. The shape looked familiar. It was . . .

**"Amy!"** shouted Allie. "What are you doing here?"

"What are *you* doing here?" Amy shouted back.

"If you are seeking answers, you have come to the right place," said Madame Lulu.

Madame Lulu held out her hand. **Clink!** Amy dropped a coin into her palm. Madame Lulu kept her hand out and looked in Allie's direction. Allie got the hint and gave her a coin too.

"Please sit down and join hands," said Madame Lulu, slipping the coins into her pocket.

★ 53 ★

"I'm not holding hands with *her*," huffed Allie.

Madame Lulu closed her eyes and rubbed her head. "I feel anger in the air," she said.

"**Ouch!** I feel it under the table," said Amy. **"She kicked me!"**

"I did not!" said Allie.

"Now, now," said Madame Lulu, trying to calm them down.

"No, not now," said Allie. "Our troubles started when Amy decided to be best friends with Gracie and not me."

"You're the one who likes Gracie best," said Amy.

**"Hold everything, girls!"** said Madame Lulu. "Why can't

★ 55 ★

you like Gracie and each other, too?"

"Well, maybe we can," said Allie. "But we can't both go to the concert with her. There's only one ticket."

"Oh, really? What concert is that?" asked Madame Lulu.

"Rockin' Rockets," said Amy.

"**Oh, I love them!** I mean, I hear they are very good, especially their new drummer," said Madame Lulu, tapping out a beat on the tabletop.

"We don't know what to do," said Allie.

Madame Lulu gazed into her crystal ball.

"The two of you are going to have to work it out together," said Madame Lulu.

"We can't," said Amy.

**"No way!"** said Allie.

"You have to," said Madame Lulu. **"The crystal ball has spoken!"**

But Allie and Amy would not listen. They each crossed their

arms and turned away from the other.

Madame Lulu gazed into the crystal ball once more. Tears filled her eyes.

"I see a sad story," she said. "I see two friends who fight. Time goes by. They don't speak to each other. They don't see each other."

"Wait! Is it me and Allie?" asked Amy.

"No. I had a best friend once," said Madame Lulu dreamily.

"She was nice. Her name was Glenda . . . or was it Brenda?"

"What happened to her?" asked Allie.

"We had a fight. A very big fight," said Madame Lulu. "And then . . . and then . . ."

"Don't tell us you stopped talking to each other! **It's too horrible even to think about!**" said Amy.

Madame Lulu moaned and threw her head back. She covered her eyes with her hand. *Clink!*

She peeked out between her fingers at the girls.

Allie and Amy looked at each other and gasped. What if the same thing happened to them? What if they really and truly never spoke again? It was definitely too horrible to think about.

"We have to go now," said Allie, jumping up.

"We have to work things out," said Amy, following her.

They dashed out of the fortune-
telling parlor.

**"Thank you, Madame
Lulu!"** they called over their
shoulders.

Madame Lulu smiled and waited a moment. Then she picked up the phone and dialed her best friend's number.

"Hello, Brenda?" said Madame Lulu, grinning. "Remember that fight we had when we were kids, and we didn't speak for three whole hours? Well, I just told two best friends the story. Of course, I **exaggerated** a little. . . ."

# 7

## Rockin' Rockets

On the way home Allie and Amy tried to come up with a plan for going to the concert together.

**"I know!"** said Allie. "We can make a costume—"

"Why?" Amy interrupted. "It isn't Halloween."

"Listen. It will be one *big* costume that two of us can fit into," said Allie. "We'll look like one person, and we'll only need one ticket."

**"That's it!"** shouted Amy. "You're a **genius**!"

"Wait. This genius just thought of a problem," said Allie. "The two of us could fit into one costume, but we couldn't fit into one seat."

"Bye-bye, genius plan," said Amy, sighing.

"Let's go to my house and think," said Allie. "There's got to be a way we can both go."

*Ring! Ring!* The phone started ringing as they walked into Allie's house.

"Who can that be?" Allie said to Amy. "It can't be you, because you're here."

"And it can't be Gracie because I know she had to go to the dentist," said Amy.

*Ring! Ring!*

"If you want to find out who it

is, you'll have to answer it," Amy said.

"Genius idea," said Allie, picking up the phone.

"Hello," said a husky voice at the other end.

"Um, Madame Lulu? Is that you?" asked Allie in amazement. Madame Lulu had never called her before!

Amy started hopping from one foot to the other. "What's she saying?" Amy whispered.

Allie listened carefully. Then

she dropped the phone and grabbed Amy's hand. "Madame Lulu got us another ticket!"

"**Yahoo!**" the girls shouted. They jumped up and down and danced around in a circle while

singing the Rockin' Rockets song "Hey, Happy Day."

"Hello? Hello!" called a voice from the floor.

"**Oops!** We forgot all about Madame Lulu," said Amy.

Allie picked up the phone again.

"Thank you very much for the ticket," Allie said, remembering her manners. "How did you manage to get one?"

"Let's just say that fortune-tellers have their ways," said Madame Lulu **mysteriously**.

"Will you be at the concert too?" asked Amy.

"I'll be there," said Madame Lulu. Then she hung up the phone.

On Friday at seven thirty Allie and Amy met Gracie and her mother in front of Peabody Palace. They were picking up the ticket that Madame Lulu had left at the box office. Allie had on her necklace. Amy was wearing the matching bracelet.

Gracie wore a GRACIE T-shirt with a big Rockin' Rockets button pinned on.

When they went inside, the Palace was buzzing with excitement. The girls followed Gracie's mother down the **aisle**.

The lights were starting to dim. As Allie and Amy slipped into their row, Allie felt something under her foot.

"Ouch!" cried a voice. It was a voice they knew all too well. It was . . .

# "MARVIN!!!"

cried Allie. "Watch where you put your feet!"

"Watch where I put my *feet*? Watch where you're *stepping*!" said Marvin. "Hey, what are you two doing here, anyway? I thought there was only one ticket."

"Isn't it amazing what highly **intelligent individuals** can do?" said Amy.

"I don't think Marvin knows very much about that," piped in Allie.

Just then Peabody Palace grew dark and the curtain went up.

There were the Rockin' Rockets, live, onstage! **The crowd went wild!**

First they heard a guitar. Then the keyboard joined in. Next the drums beat out an awesome rhythm.

*Bam, bam. Clink! Bam, bedoo-bop, bam. Clink! Clink!*

Allie and Amy turned to each other. **It wasn't possible!**

They leaned over for a good look at the drummer and saw

about twenty bracelets on each arm. It *was* possible. Madame Lulu was the Rockin' Rockets' new drummer! They caught her eye and waved. Madame Lulu waved a drumstick back at them.

"So that's how she got the ticket," said Amy. "She knew someone in the band."

"That's right. Herself," said Allie.

*Bam, bam. Bam, bedoo-bop, bam. **Clink!***

"Everyone, sing along," the lead

guitarist said into the microphone.

That was just what the kids had been waiting to hear. They jumped up from their seats and started singing:

*"Are you ready, everybody?*
*We'll be takin' a trip,*
*on the shiny silver rocket*
*called the Friend Ship!"*

**"This is so cool!"** said Amy, squeezing Allie's hand.

"I can hardly believe we're here,"

said Allie, returning the squeeze.

They went back to singing.

*"It's blast-off time!*
*Come on, take a chance.*
*Get on your feet, and*
*dance, dance, dance!"*

Marvin danced in the aisle.

Gracie bounced in her seat.

And Allie and Amy rocked with the Rockets all night long.

# Word List

**aisle (I'LL):** A walkway between rows of seats

**amazement (uh·MAZE·ment):** A feeling of great surprise

**announcer (uh·NOUN·ser):** A person who gives information in a public place

**chanted (CHAN·ted):** Said or sang words over and over again

**concern (con·SERN):** To be important to someone

**exaggerated (ig·ZA·juh·ray·ted):** Described something as greater than it really was

**exasperated (ig·ZA·spuh·ray·ted):** Showing strong feelings of annoyance

**genius (JEEN·yus):** A very smart person

**glamorous (GLA·muh·rus):** Very fancy-looking

**glaring (GLAIR·ing):** Staring angrily

**headquarters (HED·kwar·terz):**
Main office or meeting place of
a group

**individuals (in·duh·VIH·jew·ullz):**
Single humans, not groups

**intelligent (in·TEH·luh·jent):**
Very smart or able to learn easily

**mysteriously
(mih·STEER·ee·us·lee):** In a way
that isn't easily explained or
understood

**obnoxious (ob·NOK·shus):**
Extremely unpleasant

**parlor (PAR·lur):** A room used for small gatherings

**trampoline (tram·puh·LEEN):** A piece of sports equipment used for jumping up and down

# Questions

1. It's fun to be with one friend. Sometimes it's even more fun to be with two. What was the last thing you had fun doing with more than one friend?

2. Has there ever been an event that you really, really wanted to go to but couldn't? What was it?

3. Gracie invited Allie to make jewelry. She invited Amy to make cookies. If Gracie invited

you to her house, what would
you like to do together?

4. Have you and a good friend
ever been angry at each other?
What made you angry? What
did you do to feel better again?

5. Why did Madame Lulu tell
Allie and Amy the story about
Brenda? Did hearing the story
help them?

6. Do you have a favorite music
group or singer? Which group
or singer is it, and what's your
favorite song?